Transparent

Aliens Among Us

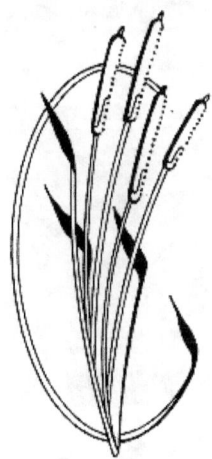

Transparent
Aliens Among Us

by Steven Lawrence Hill Sr.

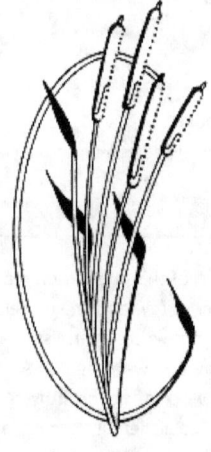

Editor
Johnathon D. Patterson

Senior Publisher
Steven Lawrence Hill Sr.

Awarded Publishing House
ASA Publishing Company

A Publisher Trademark Cover page

ASA Publishing Company
Awarded Best Publisher for Quality Books
105 E. Front St., Suite 205, Monroe, Michigan 48161
United States of America
www.asapublishingcompany.com

Copyrights©2011 Steven Lawrence Hill Sr., All Rights Reserved
Book: Transparent "Aliens Among Us"
Date Published: 09.2011
Edition 1 *Trade Paperback -volume 1*
ASAPCID: 2380564
ISBN: 978-1-886528-06-2
Library of Congress Cataloging-in-Publication Data

This book was published in the United States of America.
State of Michigan

A Publisher Trademark Title page

Transparent
Aliens Among Us

by Steven Lawrence Hill Sr.

"To the children who had to mature before their time and to the parents who's past is forgiven."

And to my very own darling children who was caught up within the alien in me.

God did not give up on me, even when I thought all was lost.

-Dad

ASA Publishing Company

ASA Publishing Company

PREFACE

Mental violence can stain an individual's mind to an unformed positive mindset when the pressures of things are going out of control in one's life. How do we deal with it, how do contain the self-enemy from within, why is there no relief valve to release from that which is inside of our thoughts?

Reckless words that course through our minds while the need to be destructive is bottling up in our heads. But how is it that God can give us a

A S A   P u b l i s h i n g   C o m p a n y

brain to pray, a choice to conquer, and the means to ignore our future's past, when we ourselves pamper the present when the ruining of our minds are held captive at bay?

This can only mean that the position in which people place themselves in and are unable to retreat from, are now forced to face the dangers of the demonic entities which lies ahead.

ASA Publishing Company

PRELUDE

"I am so messed up in my head that if I wanted to get away, I couldn't. I cannot go back into the world of my past. My past is a past of hell and demons, itching to destroy me as if I were their spiritual mark."

"You can run but you can't hide" says the demon to the soul. "I will mess up your emotions, I will mess up your life, I will mess up your family, and then I will kill you- with you! So go on, run my little spotted butterfly, run and see if I don't catch you and rip your guts out! You are no more less than the other messed up christians trying to cry to a god that you have separated yourself from.

Who are you going to cry now, you little smut-face dog! We know that you will not see heaven, because even if you think that you will get a glimpse of those pearly gates, you will only see it from a distance with those wounds that we placed on your pathetic human back. And not only will you not see heaven, but we will enjoy seeing you down here exercising those charcoaled lungs, crying out with the pain of worms that will be roaming in and out of your eye sockets. And then, there will be the heat from all of the exhaustion of your dried up tears that we will gather and blow into the abyss of these flames, in which you will be forever tormented!"

"To hell with me then, shall I go!

Why am I a stranger among my own kind?! Why is God allowing those monstrous Christians to make me feel worse than I already am? Why am I not as an important person like those who sit in tall chairs and make commands? Why did I have to leave the church, I didn't steal anything, I was just dirty.

I want to run away as far as I can, nobody loves me anymore, nobody! Just leave me to suffer my pain, for I know that is my future. I cannot go on living like this as a shadow of a man who cannot think for himself. I know what, drugs, alcohol, suicide, is my destiny. Forget mental health, I am a former Christian who just got slapped by the hand of God, and was left to die here on this planet to rot, rot, rot!"

Poor little man, what has become of him, he is deeply in pain and has no outlet for himself.

*****

As he pushes open the front door of his apartment, he runs off down onto the streets leaving his home, his wife, and his three kids, never to return again.

Years went by and one of the little children from that family has become at the age of twenty. She has a family of her own now, but she remembers when her father had left and her mother had gotten strung out. Even though as a little girl, there was something else that her and other little children had viewed as pertaining to the world in which they lived in their former past…

*****

INTRODUCTION

Part 1

Kim's father left on a mystery, only to be told bits and pieces of fables to harden up the heart of a child. Just to find out that other children were also experiencing parenting failure. As she looks back into her past, our story begins.

*****

And that is to say, "Not every rose is black, but what's inside of every child who has been losing the will to love."

Not one could explain the true epidemic of elementary kids constantly disappearing in and out of different schools. Till one day a bright young new kid entered the school by the name of Howard Johnson, begins to enlighten the other students that there was something far more sinister at work. That the parents were being possessed by aliens and the streets were filled up with shadows.

The analysis of a ten year old child, trying to grasp the concept of what has been happening within his own life with new parents and a paranoid sister, when he notices one day that when his sister tried to silently creep into the bathroom, there was this smell, a cloud of smoke, and then she came running out with her eyes beaming like she saw a ghost, and then closing the blinds of the house and starts looking for little people hiding in the closet.

The children cannot see the alien's true identity, nor the shadows only purpose until us as parents become "Transparent."

ASA Publishing Company

ASA Publishing Company

CHAPTER 1

"Hey honey, where have you been?"

"Ah, I just stopped at our usual coffee shop where we use to hang out together and sip on some French Vanilla, that's all."

"Without me? I thought that we only go there when we're together."

"Yeah, but I…"

"No buts about it! Come on

children, it's twelve o'clock at night, and you got school in the morning. As for you mister, the coffee shop closes at 10pm, and you get off work around four o'clock in the afternoon."

"That's alright, act like you're the head of the household, but I put food on the table!"

"What?! I keep your nasty toosh happy behind those close doors, and cook those meals for the few chewable teeth that you have left. That by the way, your new toothbrush is still in the package in which I bought you off of my bridge card income!"

"What?! You mocking me girl? I,I,I,...I ought to knock you upside your head. But you know what, that's okay, I'm cool with that."

Slam!!! Enraged by the seditious comments, the father exits angrily into the world of the unknown where mysterious shadows and alien possessions share a common ground.

"Mama, where's Daddy going?"

"I thought I told you and your two little brothers to go to bed."

"But Mama, I'm scared to lose a father."

"Where did you get that type of talking from? You're only nine years old."

"From some of the other kids at school. A lot of them have been complaining about the reason why they fall asleep so much in the classes. And some of the others talk about how if you are a pre-teen with no mama or daddy, you can forget your future with a real family."

"Nonsense girl, don't listen to everything you hear."

"But Mama, it's true. A lot of kids in my school are starting to get worried about the future of losing their own parents."

"Young lady, I know you care and all, but your father isn't going anywhere, and neither am I. So come on, let me tuck you in and let's have our little nightly prayers together, okay?"

"Okay. I love you Mama!"

"I love you too, my little munchkin head."

A S A   P u b l i s h i n g   C o m p a n y

CHAPTER 2

"Good morning kids. I cooked a good breakfast for you this morning."

"Mama."

"Hum, what is it daughter?"

"Did Daddy come home this morning?"

"Ah, you know what, you just missed him. I think he went to work already."

"But Mama, Daddy's briefcase is

still in the hallway where he left it last night, when he came back from the coffee shop. And what's that smell in the bathroom Mama? It smells like what that guy, you and Daddy use to bring home was smoking. I think Daddy called it a Primo."

"Go on now daughter, you're just imagining things. Hurry up and eat your breakfast, the school bus will be here soon.

"Oops! There's the bus now. Don't forget your book-bags. And make sure your brothers get on the bus with you after school, they're only in the first and second grade you know."

"I won't forget Mama, love ya!"

As the school bus door closes and little Kim sits down, she glances over to where she lives and notices that her father's car is still in the back-end of the driveway. Now she wonders if what she really heard was true, but only time will tell.

A S A   P u b l i s h i n g   C o m p a n y

"Hey Jeremy."

"Hey Kim, what's up?"

"Oh, nothing."

"I just…wait a minute Kim, did you hear about the new kid that's standing down the hallway next to your classroom?"

"No, what about him?"

"He's still trying to convince people that our parents and older sisters and brothers are getting possessed by aliens."

"Are you serious?"

"Yeah, because he claims he saw his sister was once acting normal until she went into the bathroom. Then ten minutes later, she asked him to check the closets for little people."

"For real?"

"Yes! Unbelievable huh?"

"I guess so, but my mother…"

"What about your mother?"

"Ah, nothing. Probably was a coincidence, that's all."

"Hey Kim, is there something

you're hiding from me, because I'm your boy, and you can talk to me."

"Nah, it's probably nothing. Let's get into class before we become late."

"Yeah, I know what you mean. As a matter of fact, you know Billy; well he is in the principal's office first thing this morning. Do you know why?"

"No, why?"

"Because he got a late ticket and his parents took turns whooping on him so hard, that he cannot sit down, nor stand against the wall. And I kinda overheard the nurse talking about contacting some state agency to come and take naked photos of him."

"Jeremy, that's sick!"

"I know, that what I heard thought. But that's what I heard."

"Well, let's not talk about it until lunch rolls around."

"Okay. See you at lunch."

Ringgggg!

"Okay class, are all my little

students present and seated? One, two, three, four, five,…all present and accounted for, except for Mr. William.

"I'm sorry to inform you that William will not be with us anymore."

"See, I told you." stated Jeremy.

"Keep it down class. I know we will all miss him, but he has some problems that I want each and every one of you to pray secretly for his family and his health. But don't let the school catch you praying out loud, I do not want to be transferred like Mr. Steinberg.

"Such a nice man, it's too bad that he spoke out in the defense of having prayers back. But don't worry your pretty little heads none, just do it on your own time for me, please. Thank you.

"Today, we are going to talk about…"

"Aliens!"

"Who said that?!"

"Me, Mrs. Jefferson."

"Ah, the new kid. And why did you say that?"

"Well Mrs. Jefferson…"

"That's Ms., my other half took a detour and got sixteen months."

"Sorry about the name mix up, Ms. Jefferson."

"Well go on young lad, as you were saying."

"Oh yeah, since this is a science class and we are currently studying about planets, why not talk about if there were aliens that do exist, and if they could possess people."

The room becomes so silent, that you can hear a pin drop. No-one says a word, not even the teacher. But everyone is looking at each other, wandering and the wondering of thoughts, could this be happening to our world. Could this be the explanation for the missing fathers and mothers, the sisters and brothers, the aunts and uncles, the grandparents?

And even the teacher starts secretly questioning herself.

"Wait a minute, time out! What's your name, new boy?!"

"They call me Ratboy, but my real name is Howard Johnson, but no relation to the hotel, although my family and I spent many of times living in them from place to place."

"So do you have something to share with the rest of your young peers, if you don't mind; concerning this alien invasion we keep hearing, hum?"

"Oh boy, here it comes!"

"Quiet class, let the new kid speak."

"Well, it all started when I was in the first grade and my parents bought this new home. My sister and I loved having our own bedrooms, plus separate bathrooms because you ladies…"

"Cut it out now, keep it clean Mr. Hotel."

"Call me Ratboy, teach."

"Why should we call you Ratboy?"

"I'll get to that in a moment. As I was saying, things were going great. Then one day, I started seeing ashtrays on our coffee table and strange men coming in and out of our house with these old cars with white cardboard tags, displaying numbers from the inside of the back window. Then after a few months went by, my mother started acting strangely, by sleeping late and leaving the toilet not flushed."

"Ewe! You nasty new boy."

"Well that's the truth!"

"Go on!"

"As I was saying, it was getting crazy in my home. My dad kept coming home at late hours of the night. I thought that he had a second job, but as I kept getting on the school bus, I kept seeing someone else driving my daddy's car around. I thought to myself, maybe, that wasn't my dad's car after all. But when I looked again, I noticed the fender on the right side being a little messed up, because my father had accidentally drove over my bicycle, and the metal piece of my training wheel left a deep gash mark that is very noticeable."

"Go on."

"Well later that day, my mother called up the school and told them to keep me at the principal's office until the police left the house. Till this day, I don't know why, but what I do know is, is that when my sister goes into the bathroom, she comes out with big poppy eyes, just beaming everywhere. Like if she was going to death ray something. Then she goes to our open blinds, and I'm talking about the whole entire house, and close them all. Next, she goes to the front blind and starts to peep in and out from it."

"Mr. Howard, are you sure, because you could be exaggerating a bit too much."

"I'm not lying teacher, she does

this for about two to three hours, then starts praying and goes right back into the bathroom again. So I opened the door and left, and she acted like it was normal for a first grader to walk the streets after dark. But you know what? What I found out when I was out there, that there were more kids my age, even some that had their little brother or sister still wrapped in baby towels, walking the streets. So I started hiding in those sewage tunnels because there were these shadows that comes out and picking up some of the other kids. But I kept hidden until I saw one of my parents finally coming home, my original parents that is. And to this day, if you come to see where I use to live, it looks like a ghost town with abandon buildings next to beautiful homes. And at night, it seems like monsters were coming out of those abandons buildings with these four-wheel carts. Then there are some that lays on the ground, and some that never gets up, but smells like those rotten animals that people leaves in the streets after they have been ran over a few times.

"Sounds to me like that's quite a story to tell. And I see how you got your nickname, Mr. Howard. Well class, does anyone have something similar like Mr. Howard's big fish story?"

"If my story is off your chart, then you tell us where is Mr. Jefferson, and do you know what happened to him?"

The classroom of young students gasps as they wondered how did Ratboy know about the teacher's husband.

"That's enough of that young man, I'm a grown woman, and you need to respect your elders!"

"Uh oh, seems like the new boy is starting to lose some brownie points with the teacher." said one of the classmates in the back row.

Yeah, and I think the teacher got

pinched with nervous warts." said another. "I don't think she'll be challenging the new boy that much."

"Yeah, seems like he's got a lot of experience of home life in the streets, if you ask me."

"Hey, let's gather up the gang and compare notes. I think the new boy may have something there."

"Well, should we invite him to our schoolyard powwow?"

"Yeah."

Ringgggg! "Okay class, it's time for lunch, don't forget your lunch tickets."

As the kids go outside on their lunch break, Kim notices that there are a lot of new faces, but fewer kids in the schoolyard playing. She now begins to rethink about what had happened at her house and if what the new kid said is true, then maybe, just maybe, the aliens paid her house a visit and are possessing her parents too.

Whoa, this is beginning to be a little too much for little Kim as she shakes her head and trying to snap herself back from her deep thought as to what is going on.

"Hey,… Jeremy!"

"Hello Kim."

"Where is everyone?"

"I don't know. It seems like every time we go to lunch, there are always new faces."

"Yeah, I seem to notice it too. And it's starting to creep me out. Hey new kid, I mean Ratboy!...Over here!"

Howard Johnson breaks off from his ten minutes of fame with some of the little girls from the classroom prior to the lunch bell ringing, with this cheesy look on his face as he gains popularity among his peers as the 'close encounter technician' of his time. But deep down inside, he is as frail and just as scared as any other little child his age, when strange things starts to happen in their lives that causes the little rose within them to begin its darkening trail.

"Yeah, what's up?"

"Oh nothing," said Jeremy as he starts to kick at the pebbles while looking downward wondering how Howard would react to what he is about to say. "We were wondering, what happen to your original parents?"

Then suddenly, it seems like the whole schoolyard was in vertigo through the eyes of little Kim, as she stares directly at Howard in awe, wondering if he is one of those kids that flips out every time someone mentions a relative who is not related to the one inquiring.

"Ah man, that is a hard one to swallow, but why do you want to know?" calmly stated by Howard, also known as Ratboy, which brings shock to the ears of the schoolyard listeners.

"I think we are starting to see strange things in our homes as well," said Kim.

"Well, if you tell me why my parent *change* concerns you, then I will tell you, but everything we speak about from here on out must remain a secret."

Jeremy quickly raised his head up and said, "That's including you, whoever you are. Who are you anyway?"

"I'm Robby. I couldn't help but noticed what you said about your sister in class, and that reminded me of some strange things that my grandmother was doing."

"Well, go on."

"Okay, but please don't tell anyone or I might disappear too, just like Billy. Do you swear it?"

All the kids in this group who were listening said simultaneously, "Yes, we all do!" Then comes the one voice out the bunch "Because there seems like an epidemic where we're dropping out like flies, and we are only in fourth grade," said Jeremy.

"Check this out, late last night

when I was staying at my grandmother's hotel apartment, she thought that I was in the tub, but I was still undressing and I heard some strange talking, it was faint, like if they were mumbling in each other's ears so I couldn't hear what they were discussing. Then soon after that, I smelled this burning sensation like a dollar store candle without any real fragrance, except for the stench of a candy cane.

So I slowly cracked open the door and took a peek, and what I saw broke my heart. She was on her knees with no top on, and these two shadows were cast around her where I couldn't see their faces.

I don't know what to make of it, so I slowly closed the door and sat in the tub. Gee, I never seen my grandma half naked before, but maybe I shouldn't have opened the door neither. Because, after awhile there were no more constant flickering and burning sound, but the smell of that candy cane scent was still there.

And when I finally came out, she was by the bed cussing God out while holding some objects in her hand, and then telling God that she was sorry for being the way she is. I don't know, I have never seen her act like that before."

"Really?" said Robby.

"Yes, really. And when she used to speak in this crazy gargle language, I always thought that her and God use to kick it, communicating. But now, she acts like she is so disconnected from her Christianity, that it's scaring me!"

As tears started trickling down Robby's face, he couldn't help but sniffle as he turned away from the group and holding his chest in painful sorrow.

"Robby, we are all having some tripped-out experiences, and we were supposed to be too young to go through things like this." said Jeremy.

"They must be getting possessed somehow. But how?" said Kim.

Then Howard begins to express himself, "Are the aliens using our bathrooms as a portal to travel back and forth?"

"And when people go into their bathrooms and…WHAM!...they are not who they are?" said Jeremy, as he continues.

"Uh, I don't know Robby, but what about you Jeremy, what do you think?" said Kim, reluctantly.

"Well it's possible, but where do they take our folks to in the middle of the night is what gets me. We're too young to go out after curfew. How about you Ratboy? You seem like you have access to nighttime roaming."

"Actually I don't, because I'm with new parents now. Before, my original parents…"

"Excuse me," interrupted Robby. "But why do you call them original parents?"

"If you let me explain, my original parents are the ones who brought me into this messed up world. But at the time I even thought that nothing could touch my family, I was wrong. When my mother lost her job, my dad told her to start mingling with the other neighborhood ladies that stay home to themselves, and go out with them on occasions just so that she could keep her mind off of thinking that she was losing her independence.

But later down the road, going out on Wednesday, Friday, and Saturday nights seems like that was her only means to exist."

"Well did your dad get upset?" said Kim.

"No, he started doing strange things too. Like letting his job go a few months later down the road when my mother kept giving him things in the bathroom."

"Oh, there goes that bathroom thing again!"

"Cool it Kim!"

"I'm trying, but it's too far out for me to stand here and believe that our relatives are going into the bathrooms and transforming into possessed aliens, and when they come out, they start hitting the streets!"

"Hey, don't get mad at me, most parents started out normal like mine did until the aliens came and started invading our bathrooms. One important factor is that when they do exit the bathroom, you become so much an ogre in their eyes that it's hard for them took look at you and speak in a language that you can understand."

"Yeah, ain't that the truth!" shouted a bystander, eavesdropping while being escorted to the school office, unknowing that it is now her turn to face the dilemma of being a casualty of war because her parents had suffered greatly due to those repeated alien attacks.

"Well, we better get back inside, it's almost time to go to our next class. Do you think we can still see each other until one of us disappears?"

"Jeremy, it will be alright. Don't worry yourself. This may be a bad dream that we will all wake up from."

"Easy for you to say Kim, but as for Ratboy and me, it's back to the hood where aliens run rampant. I even seen aliens driving through these streets with Lincoln's, and after a few days of their social gathering, some of them begin walking from house to house asking ridiculous questions and picking up anything off the ground that they can get their hands on.

Then after a few nights have passed, the alien control that had these people possessed decides to release them without warning and then have them slowly heading back to wherever they came from. Probably from a home with a family and kids like us. Some of them even seem to know who the shadows are and start running home."

As everyone is heading back to their class, Jeremy continues to dribble the others intellect with his new-found foresight of alien adductive knowledge through the hallway, while Ratboy is tugging on his corduroys, trying to get his attention to lower his voice down a little bit.

"One time, I saw a shadow put a cap in the back of the head of an alien because the alien tried to take something from it."

"Well, did the alien get back up?" asked Robby.

"No, it transformed back into a human again because the guy from the ambulance who was hovering over the body said that he knew him, and that he owned a business, and another person said that he heard him yell out to the shadow that he could repay him, whatever that means."

"Well how do you know that that wasn't the alien talking?"

"Because of his eyes, they weren't beaming, nor was he wobble walking like a zombie.

"Oh, hey wait. That's it!" yelled Robby.

"What's it?" hollered Kim from a distance.

"Let's start watching their transformation when it takes place, then we would know if our relatives are becoming possessed."

"But how do you snap your relatives out of the possession trance?"

"I don't know," said Ratboy. "The last time I tried to talk to my original parents, my father was digging in between the carpet looking for something, and my mom was scraping something out of this glass tube that she got from a convenient store that use to have a little rose in it. And then after she pushed this greenish black stuff from the tube, she pours alcohol on it, lights it, and begins scraping it with a razor blade and get this, she puts it right back into that very same hollow glass tube and went right back into the bathroom again. Minutes later, she came out peeking and beaming again."

"Ah, that's sad dude. I feel for you."

"Oh but wait, there's more."

"You gotta be kidding me," said Kim.

"Just listen for a second…and every time I tried to ask her something, the alien was mumbling constantly through my mother's voice. I couldn't make it out, but I think she was trying to call out for help from within. I don't know, it spooked me."

"Ratboy, you got issues!" said Robby. "But you down, we give you that much credit!" As they bumped elbows together in urban coolness.

"So, ah, what are we doing?"

"I don't know, but getting to class. The bell must have rung while we're jeeper creeping ourselves with these alien attacks."

"Oh, no. I can't go home!"

"What's the matter Robby?" said Jeremy, as the rest of them leans over to hear while shoving one another through the doorway of the classroom.

"I told you, I can't get a late ticket or I will end up like Billy!"

"Ah man, I'll take the blame."

"You will do that, Kim?"

"Yeah, what are friends for. Besides, I think you're cool."

"What?! In case you haven't noticed, I wear glasses and my grandmother dresses me up like I'm going to a funeral."

"It's church clothes, Robby."

"And Kim, if you are going to take the slack off of Robby, what are your parents going to say, huh?"

"Well Mr. Jeremy, my folks aren't that bad at this moment. They must be in the beginning stages of the possession. They're not even transparent enough to be labeled as alien infected yet."

CHAPTER 3

Three years have pass since little Kim's father left home. No one has heard from him nor seen him. But throughout those years, as far as being the victim of a possession of an unforeseen alien that has been left to trap, bound, and shackle the father's mind and body, and periodically leaving him stranded on an island of chaos; streets that contain teepee's and little boxes with fabric parts, left only for the sleepers of the noontime. For at night, they will crawl out with the stench of death, roaming as monsters, that their looks are no more hidden, but the demon from within. Robbing, stealing, and killing one another for particles of hard cotton colored dust. Frightening children as they walk by, terrorizing convenient stores with elements of surprise. They no more look normal to the average child but lost relatives that has been taken away into the night and left to die against their will from the ones they love.

*****

"Say Mr., can I borrow a dollar?"

"What, you insane, go get a job!"

"Just look at me Sir. Do you think I need help?"

"What you need is a bar of soap, a hot rag, and a clean pair of underwear. Geesh, you smell like rotten vinegar."

"Oh, you think that's funny?!"

"No, I think you're funny, now leave me alone. I'm trying to catch the bus here."

As the unwanted man starts to pull away to the opposite direction, he leans back, picks up a broken brick that is lying next to the gutter and…

SMACK! "Oh, ah, ooh!"

The alien returns and strips the man down, then takes all that he has in his pockets. The individual just lays there bleeding, gushes of blood pouring from out of his ears. Shaking and twitching with pain as he looks up and only see legs and feet running off with all he had before his eyes go dim into unconsciousness.

"What have I done?!" I didn't mean to hurt that man. Why, why, why! I cannot believe what I done. I knew I was no good. I'm just as dirty as the rest of them. My fate is no more than a pillar of salt. God cannot forgive me now. I'm no good to Him. If this is my hell that I'm living in, then the next hell will have to wait until I finish enjoying it!

No, no, no! That is not me, what is going on?! I got to regroup. I can still be good, but I left my family and I do not know just how long I've been out here. Oh, what have I done? What have I done?! I can't go back, it's too late. Ah, my head is in pain. I can't think! I gotta go find the shadows and get a recharge."

As the man who battles his demons, is far worse than before when he left home. His past haunts him with terror, his mind demonically influenced with grief. He cannot follow his own advice because he has become an alien without reason.

Each day that passes by shackles him with more pain. A man tormented beyond wisdom of this world can never regain consciousness or a thought pattern of hope. He wanders the public streets as if there wasn't a soul around. To us, he is standing in an empty room. To him, he is that empty room.

And so, as he drifts back into the foggy mist of the evening, for today he left a pool of blood and a heart of guilt. But tomorrow will be another day to lurk among the living, as little Kim's father vanishes away.

A S A   P u b l i s h i n g   C o m p a n y

CHAPTER 4

Meanwhile, in the present…

ASA Publishing Company

Ringgggg!!!

"Oh, that's the bell class! Have a good weekend, and hopefully I'll see some of you Monday." said Ms. Jefferson as she gets up from her desk, then walks towards the dry eraser board and begins wiping it in slow motion as her mind drifts into deep thought as if the only thing you could hear is the sound of the eraser in a vacant classroom.

You see, her concerns was that of what Howard Johnson (Ratboy) was saying. Every time school ends for the day, she cannot look at the children to see them off because she is afraid to really become attached to her class, knowing that there is a progression in the school with the unaccountable loss and the transferring of children that comes and goes. So, as she slowly lifts her eyes at a glance towards the doorway, as she begins to see the last

little feet exits the room, she walks over and closes the door, then sits down at one of the students' desk and then begins to weep.

Although she has no children of her own, she is now petrified as to what would become of her life if she would have had a child by the former ex-husband who is currently serving sixteen months minimum up state.

For in the back of her mind, there is a possibility that he might have been possessed before they got married because there was always something that kept a compiled focus of thought about the way her ex would frequently leave in the middle of the night when they use to live together. Then there was the smell in the bathroom and these strange shadows that he would bring into the apartment, trying to convince her that they were distant relatives and that they were musicians who needed to borrow the marble crest piano on the very next day of his payday. Another interesting thought that brings a more burden of curiosity is that they would always manage to return the piano back to the apartment complex, but it would be dropped off three doors down.

As for the bathroom, what she describes to herself verbally in a soft spoken tone when bringing back to memory,

"He would first tell me that he was going to take a shower. Then for about two hours later as the shower steam presses through the cracks of the door, I can almost hear what I thought to be clicking sounds, had crackling noises following right behind it. Then there was that candy cane odor. That smell, I cannot get rid of that smell in my mind!"

While coming out of thought, the teacher jumps up out of the seat of the student's desk where she was sitting, grabs her coat and then bolts out of the classroom as if she had just seen a ghost.

For Ms. Jefferson is about to head home and inspect the bathroom.

What the teacher is looking for, she doesn't have a clue. But what she is about to discover will play a trick on her curiosity and lead her down a dark path that may take the bravery of those little black roses like Kim and Ratboy to help bring her back. These are children who are being forced out of a natural childhood into an unknown world of maturity that wasn't meant to be dealt with for the youths of their time. Soon they will have to rise up one day and face the awful truth that their very own teacher is also vulnerable to the powers of alien possession.

*****

While the children leave the elementary compound, Ratboy walks with Kim to the school bus and Kim looks over at him and says, "Did you happen to notice what the teacher just said to us before we were leaving?"

"Nah, my mind was on what this weekend would be like. But go ahead, tell me what did Ms. Jefferson say?"

"She said that hopefully she'll see some of us Monday."

"Wow, that's creepy! What do you suppose she meant by that?"

"I don't know, maybe because our class is getting smaller. But I still got my mind set on about this weekend. Say, Kim, can I hang out with you this weekend?" said Ratboy. "I do not want to stay at my house all day with my kooky sister. Especially, if she starts acting weird again when she comes out of the bathroom.

Remember my old parents, now I'm starting to think the aliens got a hold of my sister too, and soon wants to take me out also!"

"Get a grip on yourself, Ratboy! Sure you can come over, but please do not mention anything about aliens in my house. I don't want my house jinxed, okay?!"

"Okay, but if I see someone come out of your bathroom with big poppy eyes beaming death rays, I'm running! And I encourage you to run with me to the sewers."

"Whatever Ratboy, whatever. Just don't forget to ask your parents for permission, and here's my address."

The school is now empty, loose papers flying through the schoolyard, cans and bottles making clanging noises as they roll down the empty streets where the buses had deployed from. Wind beating on the glass of the school windows as little mice's come out onto the hallway floors to signify that school has officially ended for the weekend, awaiting to be stirred once more when the next school day rolls around.

CHAPTER 5

Three years into the future, the badly affected father of little Kim is on a rampage of a tormented soul. Mentally withered, he sees no opportunity of escape but to endure the suffering as a man who only dreams of a faded reality in which he once had.

"Ah, why do you seek to destroy me? I cannot take the violence that's waging war in my head. Too many complications to think! My pain, my growing pain. Is there more to this then life? It seems like every turn for me is the wrong avenue. People trying to tell me what to do as long as it benefits them. Even my wife got pregnant by another man while I was still with her. How could she do this to me? And now hoe-hopping with my brother? Oh no, I have to be the bad man in their little eyes as my children thinks that I have abandoned them? Oh, what sorrow that is in our mist. They're growing into a world of fantasy lies against me. The pain of knowing without really knowing; the secrets!"

His rambling continues as he sits in a Catholic Church bathroom while continually being struck with the demonic attacks that enhances his possession. "I wish I could express to my children just how much I love them, but looking into the eyes of one of my children and seeing another shadowed parent lurking from inside curls my stomach to vomit. And although I love "them, I just cannot look at the one who bare them any longer, nor will I be able to see trust in a woman again.

God! Is there somebody for me that I can love? Do I have to continue to look at the stars at night and cry? Do I still have to see their little faces, the images of the day when I left? For one is not mine, and you knew this."

The alien possession is so severe that this poor man is liable to do anything to stop the pain. Apparently, he is torn between the two faces of himself. One of who he was, and the other that's taking him for a joyride to hell continues to lead him to his own self destruction. Griping and complaining, now he is back to blaming God for his demise. Trying to feel like Job and yet, no real companions for the journey as he continues to torture himself.

"They knew it, everyone else

knew it, and I only had suspicion. Yes, and it has came to past. Therefore, I am deeply in sorrow. Sure, I'll take whatever is being dished out at me! I don't care anymore. I cannot believe that I stand alone against my brother's treacherous lies, and my ex's whorish ways. To hell with me! I shall rot on this day, and this time forth! I am not loved, but shall be despised and hated with the grim looks and evil imaginable thoughts that lurk in every faded light. Even Peter's shadow cannot heal me, for mine is too dark.

There is no movement of positive motivation but destruction and an eight by ten padded cell calling out my name. I shall roam the earth with the stench of defeat. For I have lost the battle of sanity, the comfort of a family, and the disappearance of a God, who my own parents believed in and yet got divorced. Now my father is dead and I've lost the will to function as a human being. Where is this God at now, who widows me against my family! I cannot go on living in a world that mimics that "nice guys do finish last!" I have to create a new world for myself. But until then…say, I like Chinese food. Please don't throw that away. At least not in the dumpster, my blanket is in there. And besides, I'm kinda hungry too."

A tormented father, pain driven by the elements of his past life as a family man who's comfort of security has been violated by the witchcraft of demonic attacks. Alone in this world, eating out of dumpsters and pushing shopping carts with the belongings that he has inherited while roaming homelessly and helplessly throughout the streets. His mind is barred with the painful question of "why." Burning the Holy Grail of his internal soul with drugs, alcohol, and repeated suicide attempts, leaving only scars that are afflicted as external wounds to carry on the old tradition of death, while internally flickering the agony of a deeper darkness.

Perhaps his fate relies in the black rose in him on how he lived as a child, where violence roamed the streets of his time. Alcohol being the hidden momentum for the animosity his family went through when he was growing up. Just could it be that his love as a child was secretly growing cold, while as an adult, searching in overdrive in order to feel loved? Where did his destruction begin to end his life? Was he in denial of what he has seen in his elementary years? Or is he torn apart with different personalities, hidden in the conflicts of battle?

Now he has accepted death and became friends with the devil. But the devil has left him stranded on a mental island where demons are to keep him at bay. Will he ever pull through and return to the promises of a better life? Or will he continue to condemn himself and all those around him who are frantically bewildered by his presence?

His life, what does it mean to him but a meaningful relationship to the environment of his surroundings. Hustling, smoking, getting high, getting drunk, pushing shopping carts, eating out of dumpsters, living in and out of jail. But he cannot ever hear that sound, the sound of trumpets rumbling around his walls. Seven times over and even seven times more, again and again, to shatter that which is internally stern and was left hardened by the virus which plagues his heart.

For the time of his clock has come to a halt. He, himself is convinced that this is the future on which he is now living. But one day, if by that chance of hope, that a mysterious presents may repossess this empty black rose and remove the biblical Job like qualities that he have come so well known to suffer. For a rose is still a rose, even if it loses its fragrance.

CHAPTER 6

Let us return to the present day where a storm in the life of Ms. Jefferson is about to begin.

School is out for the weekend and she has arrived at home quite earlier than expected because of her sudden curiosity concerning the bathroom in her apartment, but what she encounters will soon bring a close connection to her students.

"Where are my keys? Oh great! I must have left them in the car. Thank goodness that my driver window is still rolled down."

While the teacher, Ms. Jefferson, walk back to the stairs of the apartment complex, she notices that the relatives of her former ex is yelling at this lady at the corner of the street and calling her out her name and continuing with a loud hatred voice yelling, "Where's the money?!" as they become more and more demanding. The attention became so obvious that it drawn a vertigo effect where the teacher couldn't help but stare while trying to put the right key into the keyhole of her complex's door.

Then there were these loud sounds as she returns back her focus on opening the apartment door.

"BLAM, BLAM!" roaring through the streets with one of those sounds muffling into silence as it penetrates deeper into its target. But the school teacher pretended like she didn't hear the gunshot rounds, especially that last bullet firing off into the human skull of the current now deceased woman. Startled by what she observed and tried unsuccessfully not to hear, she jumped in panic and dropped her keys onto the base of the top of the stairs, not looking back to see if anyone was coming.

Now afraid, she is trying to shake off just the thought of someone getting executed in front of where she lives is destroying her nerves. Let alone, those thugs that happen to supposedly be her ex husbands relatives, make it even more difficult to figure out. So as she finally got into her apartment, she threw her purse and coat down onto the floor and went towards the coffee table to grab herself a cigarette. For she is still shaking badly through so much intense nervousness, that the adrenaline which is pumping through her veins is driving her mind immensely wild about what she thought she had heard, and yet willingly not wanting to question the event that just might take her over the edge. Then suddenly, there's a knocking at the door…Rat-Tat-Tat!

"Mrs. Jefferson, is your husband home? We need to borrow the piano again."

"Not tonight, I'm tired."

"Mrs. Jefferson, open the door, it's your husband's relatives."

"Sorry, he left me! But you can find him up state."

"How far up state?"

"About sixteen month's worth."

"Ah, sorry about that Mrs. …"

"That's Ms. now. And I want to be left alone for awhile, alright?"

"Whatever you say, Ms. J."

A sigh of relief for the moment for Ms. Jefferson, the teacher who is already on a nervous edge, with an implanted thought from what one of her students had mentioned. But as she winds down with puff after puff, she starts becoming focused as she leans back onto her sofa and stares at the bathroom door, just a few feet down the hallway in her voluptuous apartment.

After a few minutes had passed and about two and a half butts, she crushes down her third cigarette into the ashtray and begins to proceed down toward the bathroom. But then, there came this ambulance sound and flashing red lights causing a glare splintering an array of colors through her window and protruding down the hallway walls, enough to stop her for a pause moment, and causing her to slowly creep towards the window. And sure enough, the ambulance workers were helping putting the body into the coroner vehicle while the police was marking a territorial area for an investigation.

After she stepped back a little from the window, she slightly sat on its ledge and began gasping for air.

"Oh my gosh! What am I going to do? Nothing! Just keep calm and act like it didn't happen. Oh my gosh! How can this happen in my own neighborhood? I just got home!!! Please, oh please, don't let those people come knocking on my door again. What kind of relatives are these people to my ex? I knew something was wrong!"

As soon as she regains control of her senses, she then turns her attention back towards the bathroom, gets up and proceeds to slowly head that direction once again. This time it would seem like a long journey down the hallway with the bathroom door pulsating with the rhythm of her heartbeat. Then once again, at that splendorous moment of curiosity, as she begins grabbing the knob of the door…

"Knock, knock, knock!"

"Oh, No! Oh my gosh, oh my gosh! What shall I do? Okay, okay. I need to get a grip on myself. God, I am so scared! I do go to church once a month, and I do pay my tithes when you want me to, and I am a good teacher to the kids, so why me?! What have I done to deserve this?"

The teacher quickly lights up another cigarette, then she goes directly to the door, opens it, and…what? It was the elderly lady that stays next door to her. She was just checking to see if she is alright. The school teacher forgot that this little old Christian woman always come like clockwork to check up on her ever since her husband never came back after hanging around with his so-called relatives.

"Is everything alright, Mary?"

"Yes, Ma'am."

"Are you sure? I was wondering if those people your husband use to hang around with is still bothering you."

"Why you ask that?"

"Well, seemingly while you were at the school, they were circling like vultures around your apartment for some reason."

"Really?"

"Yes. In fact, look at the bottom of your door. It looks like someone kicked it out of anger."

"Wait a minute Miss Green, how do you know so much about everything?"

"Well, if you get to be my age,

there's nothing new under the sun. It seems like old history likes to take on new volunteers to carry out its dirty work. But if you ask me, I think your ex brought the devil with him! Yeah, if he just stops messing with those shadows, he wouldn't be getting so possessed all the time."

The elderly lady Miss Green turns away from the door as she wobbles back to her apartment. If you listen closely, you can hear a faint mumble as she recalls some of the memories of her very own experiences. Ms. Mary Jefferson looks bewildered within her own recollection of one of her students, Ratboy, had said to everyone in the Science classroom as she looks at Miss Green wobbling down the hallway and into her own apartment.

As both doors close, one after the next, you can hear a pin drop as the rumbling noises of the hallways in the complex quiets down for the evening. No more yelling, not even the sound of sirens, nor were there any children in the streets to be found. Only the police and the investigators to a homicide that this bright skinny young school teacher and her sporty little squared reading glasses, refuses to accept that hell will soon enter into her world and change the lifestyle that she thought she was accustomed to.

For tomorrow is another day that will compel her curiosity, an emotion that is mentally tampered with, with the decisions to explore a portal that transforms careless individuals into those flock of aliens who's eyes are bugged, their bladder is uncontrolled, and their paranoia brings shadows that engulfs the decisions between right and wrong. All by the exchange of this shiny little object, the key to which all madness has no reasoning.

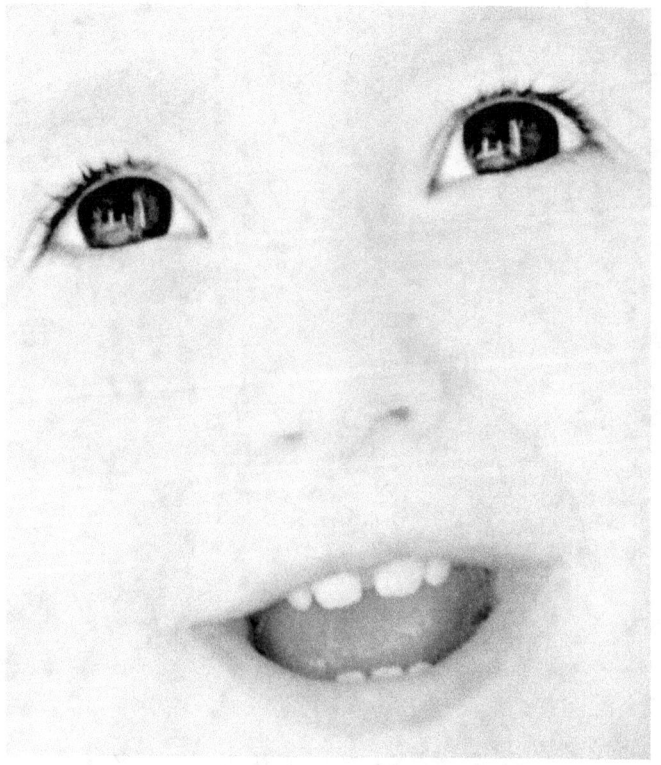

There are times when we do not look through the portal eyes of a child, till one day the children of our past has come to develop their own conclusion, that their parents are being possessed by aliens.

A S A   P u b l i s h i n g   C o m p a n y

It's Saturday morning, and Ratboy has been discovered hiding in the bushes in the front yard of Kim's house. Her father has not come home yet, and the school teacher is just waking up from a horrible night only to find out that her bedroom window was left cracked open, and a butter-knife is lying on the carpet, directly underneath the window seal.

A S A   P u b l i s h i n g   C o m p a n y

Little Kim's Father

Part 2

ASA Publishing Company

A S A   P u b l i s h i n g   C o m p a n y

THE SETTING

"Hey, Poppy. What can you do with this?"

"What you got?"

"A ladies Rolex."

"Not bad. How much?"

"Oh, about fifty."

"I'll give you fifteen."

"Auh, you killing me man. Come with it…whoa, whoa, whoa! What you giving me man?!"

"This is what you want isn't it?"

"Nah, I just want the money."

"Yeah, sure. But we all know where you're going, right?…To the land of the paranoids."

"Kiss my juicyfruits, and give me my money."

"Don't get soar at me because you need some zoom-zooms and wham-whams! Here take it, and you better go on before I let Hector loose on you! And close the gate on my fence when you leave!"

"Ah, what the heck."

(*A silent whisper in the ears of a four legged juggernaut*) "Hector. Go sick'em boy."

As little Kim's father slowly closes the gate, a violent sound of four paws pouncing its prints through the unseeded gravel as the dirt bounces up into the air by the mighty force of strength. He then begins to leap forward, towards its victim of prey, only just to get one of his paws caught in the locking clamp of the gate. All the mean while, Kim's father is mumbling to himself, not realizing that if it were just a few seconds a little too late, he would have had sharp pointed fangs protruding through his left hand, while glancing down at his right hand that was still trickling with blood.

"I can't believe I cut myself with that dog-gone butter-knife." As Kim's father continues to mutter.

A S A   P u b l i s h i n g   C o m p a n y

THE PRELUDE

It's Saturday morning, and Kim's father had been up all night trying to find a lick somewhere, where he could make some money while trying to subdue the internal feign from within, that causes one to lose oneself from a normal coherent state of mind.

A S A Publishing Company

INTRODUCTION

Part 2

As little Kim's fathers' craving grows stronger, his ability to comprehend grows weaker. He will now take that plunge into becoming no more than what he had feared the most, a little spotted butterfly, as the hovering demons continue to verbally torment him with.

Although a butterfly seems to be beautiful; as one who has just been delivered by the "Blood of the Lamb," a Christian man who has fallen into a backslidden state usually goes back to those with negative influences once a place of worship closes the door in a person's heart. Because life and death are in the power of the tongue, and those that love hearing what we say, might eat the fruit that we dish out. For its sad that one might not see the sinner who was saved by grace.

CHAPTER 7

"Blink! Blink! Blink! Blink! Blink!"

"Click!"

"Ah man, what a long night."

Mrs. Mary Jefferson had a rough night experiencing a homicide that she is willingly wanting to ignore, but the concept of her ex-husband having so-called relatives that performed an execution in the street, then coming to her door and asking to borrow the piano, is beyond all reasoning.

"I guess I'll go ahead and take me a nice hot bath. But first, a little hot cocoa and a ciggy should awake my morning coma."

While little Kim's school teacher, Ms. Jefferson remains sitting on the bed contemplating whether she should run her bath water prior to having a cocoa and cigarette bliss, she notices that her curtains are flapping slightly open, as the morning breeze whisk its dampness onto her knees, causing her to buckle a little.

(*While closing her robe*) "It's a little nippy. But how can that be, all the windows are closed."

As she got up and walked towards the location of the breeze, she steps right on a butter-knife that was lying on the floor, almost just below the window seal.

"What's this? And there's dried blood on it….hum. Wait a minute, my window is partially open. What the?! No, un ah! You mean to tell me that someone was in here while I was sleep? I've had enough within 24 hours. It's time to move."

"We don't think so Ms. Jefferson, but you can come with us down to the station."

"Who the heck are you, and how did you get in here? And how dare you come into my bedroom! Get Out!!! I've had enough excitement, and it's not even lunchtime!"

"Ah, we're from the 34th District Crime Unit…." (*As they pause with slow caution,*) "….Homicide."

Sadly to say, she is now involved. Whether voluntary or involuntary, she is a witness and will probably have to testify. But how far will she go to let them know that there is more paradoxes in the mist that has lucrative connections; ties with her ex, and whoever broke in the…

"Where's my watch?! Oh, sugar, honey, ice, tea!!!"

"Ma'am, what did you just say?"

"Nothing, just nothing."

"Ma'am, are you okay?"

"Yeah, I think."

"You think? What do you mean by that? Is there something that we need to know?"

"No,…why?" Loosing mental balance, she looks around the room pausing with hesitation.

"Just routine probing,…ah I mean, checking."

As the officer cleverly trickles her nerves, he begins to observe her reactions and movements. But the only thing he notices is that she seems to be holding a butter-knife in her hand. And get this, it has dried blood stains on it!

The officer in front of the school teacher immediately pulls out his revolver and quietly signals another officer in back of her, to glance at what she has in her hand. Then with a quick draw, out comes a tazer. The officer in front then yells at the top of his lungs with this loud voice...

"Drop the weapon!"

An echo from all the other officer's that just walked in..."drop the weapon! Drop the weapon!"

Then all of a sudden, as soon as she jumps up in the air, due to the fear and the panic of the multiple verbal tactics...zzzzzzzap! Tazered right in the lower collarbone.

"What did you do that for?"
"Because you signaled me."
"Idiot! I just wanted you to be on alert!"
"Oh, okay!"
"Too late now Rookie!"
"Then what about her? Should I

handcuff her while she is out?" As he snickers.

"Out? Can't you see that she is still shaking? What level setting do you have it on?"

"Low."

"Low? Knucklehead, release your hand off the trigger and get in the car!"

"Ah, man! I know her." As another officer approaches the sprawled-out body.

"She is a very respectable elementary school teacher in this community. It's a shame that we had to send her husband upstate for that accessory to murder; vicious attack on some guy trying to catch the bus awhile back."

Then a female officer replied, while pulling out an investigation form and began thinking about other events that took place at the very same bus stop. "Gee, we never did catch the one that had hit the deceased with a broken piece of brick. But sooner or later, he'll make a mistake. But in the meantime Sir, what about her?"

"Oh, yes. Officer McClemick, please pull the points of the tazer out of her shoulder, and put everything back like it was,…and you know what, leave the butter-knife."

Officer Danielle McClemick looks at the Lieutenant in astonishment as he ponders his diabolical thoughts like one who committed a crime. But she did as she was told to do without question.

The Lieutenant looks back at the officer and shakes his head from side to side, then holds up his index finger as if to *say just one moment while I compile my thoughts*, then he continues. "The homicide was due to severe head shots at point blank range. And there was no evidence of a stabbing that had taken place. Besides, good o'le knucklehead here would cause us a massive lawsuit if she were to press charges when she wakes up. People had seen us come in the building and roaming across the sand outside in back of her window, but no-one saw us come into this apartment."

More and more, the Lieutenant is bringing on unnecessary drama into the investigation part of the crime scene, and Officer MClemick will not dismiss this as an accident, but only for now.

"Okay Sir. You heard what the man said people. So let's get this place together."

But only if they knew, that the little old Christian woman, Miss Green, who was just a little ways down the hall, had her door cracked open, peeping and listening for personal memoir to exploit if she needed to use that bit of information whenever a situation arise.

In the meantime, Mrs. Jefferson is regaining consciousness and rubbing her shoulder, as it appears that she has been placed back on her bed.

But one thing is different; she is

holding the butter-knife, once again.
Hum…

CHAPTER 8

Just two blocks away in an alley, from where the police had just left, aliens were running rampant. Some were walking around with no clothes on while others were still half naked and on their knees, scraping between the grooves of the concrete. Some were using long thin pointy shiny objects, and others were just using their fingernails. What were they searching for, you got me, but it definitely was a buck wild display of hardcore alien possession. It would seem like the same people that we use to know, had gotten totally influenced somehow.

"Mama!"

"Go on child. You don't know me. I'm not your mama!"

"Yes you are! Let go my mama, alien!"

"I said, I'm not your mama!" as she pushes the child away.

Tears trickling down the possessed parents face as the alien gains more control. But for a brief moment, the mother starts to reach her hand towards her son in a passionate glimpse of a child that she had left behind for another to adopt from the shame of mental torment that she had left this child starving and barely breathing, cold and unwanted, when one day she left out of her bathroom and took this child out into the night, to never return home again. For it was Howard Johnson (Ratboy), who while running frantically out the alleyway, couldn't bear to look back. His heart was becoming more destroyed by this unforeseen mystery, that stricken a parent's mental capacity to acknowledge that they have a responsibility to the pitty-patter of little feet that carries a smile when looking up and saying those words of what families are made of, *I love you*. But instead, a rose cannot blossom if the gardener is taken on a detour from his, her, their duties as a parent. Don't lose that fragrance Ratboy, there is still hope!

But in the meantime…

"Say girl, get back in here and take another blast. This will stop those precious tears."

"I don't know, I just don't know. What the hell am I still doing here! That was my son!"

"I know the feeling girl. I have a daughter and two younger boys, but I'm trying to put it all past me. You see, when I gave up, I just sat my briefcase down in our hallway at home and jetted. I just could not forgive what my wife had done to me. The pain was so great, that the doctor's couldn't cure me on those hourly visits. They go home and I'm stuck reminiscing about the horrors that I was trying to forget. But I gotta tell you, taking this blast, and my mental troubles are over. It's almost like an *out of body* experience. I just hate it, when I have to float back down into reality. But to me, this here, what we're doing, is reality. So take this blast before I get upset."

"Excuse me?!"

He slapped her. She slapped him. He busted her in her grill. She kicked him in his groins.

"Ah, that's the spirit! You feel better now? Because I don't. You just blew my high. Well, gotta go find another lick."

"You're not gonna leave me out here by myself, are you?"

"Naugh, just find someone to kick it with until I come back."

Little Kim's father walks off into the streets. It is now 12pm in the afternoon; visible to the world. He has no shame, nor remorse about what he has become, a person with an unusual transformation that changes the way one thinks. A clown type figure changing form and roaming through the streets trying to make a hustle, just to maintain the pleasures of the alien abduction from within, who will soon become the mystery behind the shiny object, a shadow.

A reflection of once was a father, but now a fugitive and a vagabond being allowed to roam the streets like Cain.

But why?

Why would God allow such people to continue to run a course of debauchery? Perhaps within God's viewpoint, there is still a little good left in the individuals like that. And not that He sees them as mindless souls, but the one's that has not backslidden so far yet as to there is no point of return.

But in those highways and byways, alleys and condemned buildings, there are some that still huddle together as if they remember what it felt like to be loved. And then there are some that has gotten so far into the possession, that their paranoia has them pretending to be fearful door servants to the little people that they see and hear, by opening and closing the draped down fabric that covers the front of their cardboard box homes. And others that cuts peepholes through their tents, to feel the sense of surveillance security, to protect them from the monsters that lurk and prey on their fragility, when their minds turn into mush after the alien possession.

$$*****$$

Now, little Kim's father is a living and breathing dead man, walking amongst the world. Zombified by the betrayal of himself. For his actions has brought him low self-esteem and careless causes, things that produces repercussions. Because sooner or later, he will have to answer for all that sowing, that he had put out on that thin little pathway he is treading.

$$*****$$

CHAPTER 9

"Say man, where you going? I see you've been out here awhile, walking back and forth." asked Kim's father.

"Why, you looking?"

"Looking for what? Because you don't want what I'm looking for."

"Try me!" Stating a challenge from the alien possessed man.

"Alright, a lick…you know what that is?" said Kim's father.

"I smell pig up in this piece!"

"Naugh, you just smell the crack of my…"

"Let's go then Beavis!"

Not more than five seconds, these two knuckleheads were on their way to do some dirt. Kim's father just didn't care who he tag team with, as long as he achieved his agenda for that hour; explaining the procedure on how he would perform this so-called easy lick that could test a person's ability to fly.

"How good are you at climbing drainpipes?" asked the alien possessed man.

"Well considering that I only weigh about a buck-fifty, I'll say I've done my Batman tricks pretty well."

"Okay Beavis the smelly Batman, I'm gonna see what you're made of."

"Yeah, okay. I hear you talking, but if you keep that name calling up, we will soon find out who has been out here the longest!"

"Yo, chill man. I'm just hanging

out on a mission with you, that's all. I'm not trying to move your grooves."

"Alright, it's cool Dawg."

"I tell you what, here's a peace offering before we continue this mission you are leading us on."

Unknowledgeable to whom he is with, did Kim's father know that that person is going to set him up once he completes his mission. So he pulls out a small piece of insurance and said, "Hit this."

And like most wind-downed and still possessed craving aliens, he pulls out his little glass tube with a colorful rose in it that he was saving for after his lick with cork still plunged together on each side, takes it apart, and then throws what he doesn't use and slap it together with a charcoaled Choy-Boy, and...*ZOOOOOMMMMM!* Now he's at a sea level hearing state of mind.

"Yo, Dog! You okay? Can you hear me?"

While Kim's father is trying to

shake off some of its effect, Beavis is truly becoming that butt-head.

"I'll tell you what, you just take yourself on to whatever you came from, and I'll handle the lick. By the way, where is that lick that we were walking to?"

"Ah, ah, ah, wait a minute, I got something clogging my nose."

Crack!!! (*A left-hand punch right to the face*) Kim's fathers' head has been forcefully twisted towards the left by that blow and down onto the pavement he bounces off.

"Is your nose clear now Dawg?"

"Yeah, it's clearing up now butt-wipe!"

"Crack!!!" (*Another left-hand to the face while he is on the ground*)

"Are you done?"

"No!"(*Punch, slap, kick, and shove*) "I'm about done now, Dawg."

"Good. Can 'WE' now get there?"

The possessed alien was so amazed that Kim's father didn't knee-up, that he started to smile like he was really his street dog. So, he didn't question him about where they were going, nor was he thinking about setting him up anymore. All he could focus about was Kim's fathers' coolness during his beam on. But don't let that fool you, some alien possessions got real game control, especially when the alien inside then know that they need roughneck sidekicks to get certain jobs done without folding in at the last moment.

"Ah, here we are!"

"What?! Get the #*0@# out of here!"

*****

Here they are, standing in the back of a police station, glancing up at an open fifth story window with a water drain barely clamped to the side of the building in broad daylight. Now if you asked me, I think those were trauma blows to his head. I don't think he needs to be trying to catch this lick. Oh, no, auh aun! He needs to be lying on a soft cushioned bed, somewhere in the Belleview Hospital and not trying to swell his chest up on this one. But hey, Kim's father got me even curious.

*****

"Are you sure you're alright? I can knock you completely out now, and throw a rock at one of these windows and run, leaving you here looking stupid."

"For your information that is the janitorial room." said Kim's father.

"How did you know that?"

(*The commentator*) "Yes, how did you know that?!"

"Man, lookie here. I'll show you. Once I go up there, I'm going to be throwing down mad cheddar-cheese licks up in this pa-zi-zow!"

"What?! You're insane!"
"Watch me."

CHAPTER 10

"Excuse me sir, what time is it?"

"Oh, about 2:17pm."

"Thanks."

"Why, you're thinking about leaving early? You know you still have to mop the Investigator Office on the third floor."

"I know boss, but I just want to know what time it is, that's all. Besides, it helps me to know that I may still have extra time to take out the trash on certain days."

"Oh, okay. Carry on."

(*Commentator*) "Oh, give me a break!"

As the janitor pushes his mop bucket across the wet floor on to the janitor's room, he looks back at the officer to make sure he went into the elevator. Then, he opens the room after the coast is clear, and bellows out bird calls through the shades of an open window.

"There's our queue."

"What queue?" said the man who is starting to come out of his alien possession.

Kim's father just looks at him with this dumdum expression, and proceeds up the drainpipe with his bare hands clamping onto its old cast iron tubing, like a squirrel searching for his last supper in the frost of winter.

"I thought you were going to let me climb?"

"I thought so too, but now you're just loud. So can you be a little more discreet and catch this computer?"

"What computer?"

(*Whoosh...Smack!!!*) Right as he was looking up.

"That computer. Payback's a 'B' huh? Now who's Beavis of this smelly Batman?!" as he looks at the blood on his shirt from getting punched earlier.

Vengeful tactics of a man who once was a white collar worker, a real shirt and tie man. And now a prodigal pillar of salt, he has left not only his briefcase in the hallway of his home, but his dignity as a backslidden Christian with so much hatred, that his self morals now has no value in life itself.

Where does he go from here but to a dark place within his heart. Losing all sense to the reality of his former life, a man who is bent on a mission to satisfy the appetite of the demonic pleasures that has seared the subconscious depths of his soul, a monster which emerges once called upon to perform those task on what it needs to feed, as it is stalking the streets, preying as a feign.

"Pisss, yo man, what you doing down there?" speaking at a lower tone from the janitor that is leaning out from the widow.

"Nothing, I had to get rid of some extra dead weight, that's all."

As the janitor backs away from the window, Little Kim's father grabs onto the window seal, and then thrusts himself through while his shoulder is grazing the blinds, causing the crackling noises of those shades.

"What are you doing? Are you insane? You can get us both caught. And not only that, you can cost me my job. Go back man!"

"Naw, I can't go back."

"What do you mean, you can't go back? It's simple, just take your nasty behind back out that window…are you alright?"

"Sorry   Dawg,   I   was flashbacking."

"Man, you ought to go back home. You got a family that you left behind."

"Right now, I just don't want to talk about it. Can we just continue?"

"Continue what? Because you have never come up in here before, and we usually square off at the bus station. Now you're twisting our normal routine around. What gives?"

Little Kim's father looks at him with this sad but fiendish eyes and shrugs his shoulder while slowly nudging him as he exits the janitorial room and enters the hallway. Not a sound bellied through the corridors, while he places these turns of unexpected events on an old friend.

As he passes the bulletin board, he doesn't notice that one of the *missing persons* pictures is actually him that was taken from a little girl wanting to find her father.

*****

His head looking down towards the floor tiles in shame, he comes to the third office door on the left, pulls out a key and opens it.

"What are you doing, man? I thought that you wanted me to continue handing you *your own stuff* out the window. But now I see that you are on one heck of a trip-out."

"To tell you the truth, I just wanted to sit at my desk one more last time, that's all."

"That's all?!"

Little Kim's father squats down in his chair and swivels back and forth with his hands propped behind his head while leaning back.

His friend softly speaks back. "Dude, I know that you are hurting each time you wind down, but sometimes when we mess up, we just have to snap ourselves back into reality. You didn't lose your job as a detective, but there is someone temporarily in your place. And guess what, he is investigating on that lick we pulled at your daughters' school teacher's apartment."

Suddenly, he looks up at his old friend and grabs him by the shirt collar and pulls him within breath-to-ear distance and says, "If I ever catch you bringing that up again, your face will have more than just a computer imprint like Beavis that butt-wipe outside in back."

"Alright man, it's your world."

"You damn right it's my world, and you best not forget that!"

"Say bro, I think this is where you and I need to depart."

"Alright, then step off!"

He then slowly releases his grip from the shirt collar of his former friend or shall we say, precinct co-worker, and at the same time he is sliding open the center drawer of his desk with the other hand.

Then all of a sudden…Slash!

Right across the neck.

"All man, what am I doing?! I'm sorry, I'm sorry!"

Blood spewing out his neck as he is pressing his clothing up to the open wound; now slouching against the wall, and slowing dropping to the floor, leaving a trail of bloodstains spattered abroad.

CHAPTER 11

"Honey, go check the mail, its eleven o'clock and the mailman has been arriving early these past two weeks."

"Okay, Mama."

It's Saturday Morning and little Kim goes out to the mailbox in front of the driveway to retrieve the mail, and when she starts returning back into the house, she notices a slight movement of the bushes. As she comes closer, she begins to hear tears of sadness. It was the soft whimpering sound of a little 10 year old trying to cope with what he saw.

"Ratboy! Are you alright? Come out of there and let's get you inside."

She extends her hand as he clasp on to be pulled up, and they both walk in.

"Mama. I have a friend from school, his name is Howard. Can he visit me for awhile?"

"It's alright with me, but don't you have to ask your father first...." She pauses with a downplay of sadness that she forgot that he still haven't returned home after a little over 6 months. "Ah, go on girl. It's alright. Ask your friend would he like to have some lunch."

"Would you like to? Then when you feel a little bit more comfortable, you can tell me what the problem was." said Kim.

"Okay. And tell your mother I said thank you."

"Not a problem."

Kim smiles at Ratboy with warm care in her eyes. "Just make yourself at home."

After they finished enjoying their lunch, they went out into the backyard and sat on the swings. During this time, the mother was having memorabilia issues in her bedroom, looking at the pictures of her husband while dabbling the mist of cologne in the air to catch his manly scent that draws those moments of passion.

Out of her sorrow, she quickly runs into the bathroom while the kids are out back, and reaches under the ledge of the sink and grabs a hold of a broken antenna, then turns the shower on.

"Hey Kim?"

"What?"

"Isn't that little window in the back of your house a portal to the tub?"

"I guess so, but you're making it sound like my house is a spaceship. Stop doing that."

"Well, there is steam forcing its way out. Is your mother okay?"

"Yes. Now will you stop that?!"

"I'm not doing anything. I was just asking."

"Well then, ask something else."

"Okay. Where is your father? Is he at work? I heard that he is a detective."

"Nah, I think he took the day off." Kim was afraid to tell Ratboy the truth that she thinks that her father was abducted as well, since it has been over six months. In the meantime, her mother is curled up in a ball on the bathroom floor, mumbling to herself.

"So Ratboy. Tell me what got your huggies blooming."

"I saw my mother today."

"I thought that you normally go home to see your parents after school."

"No, I mean my real mother!"

"Oh, where?"

"You don't want to know, Kim."

"Go on, I'm here for you."

"Well, okay. I saw her in an alley with a bunch of half naked aliens."

"Come on, are you serious?"

"Look, if you don't believe me, come look for yourself. But I'm afraid to look down that alleyway again and see more of the final chapter of my real family."

"No matter what you want to do, I'm right here for you."

In the back of Kim's mind, she was thinking that could it be possible, that her father was possessed and drawn into this alleyway also.

"You know what, let's go round up the gang and then we'll all catch the bus to Ms. Jefferson's apartment and I'm sure she will go with us. It's always good to have an adult who is not under the influence."

Epilog

TRANSPARENT 2

"Murder in the 34th Precinct"

There was a murder committed in the former detective's office but there wasn't a body to be found. Officer Danielle McClemick discovers the picture on the bulletin board was that of the detective. Howard Johnson and little Kim is about to pay the school teacher a surprise visit to travel on the darkside of town. Ms. Jefferson discover marks on her body and a butter-knife in her hand while lying in bed. And a new kid will be rescued from an abandon building swarming with monsters, who will soon be introduced into the fold by the name of Scooter.

ASA Publishing Company

www.ingramcontent.com/pod-product-compliance
Lightning Source LLC
Chambersburg PA
CBHW071130250626
47159CB00006B/2191